Rough-Face

A Native American Cinderella Tale

CHARACTERS
IN ORDER OF APPEARANCE

Storyteller

Nootau
Rough-Face Girl's father

Invisible One
a special being

People of the village

Kanti
a girl of the village

Kimi
a girl of the village

Nadie
Invisible One's sister

Tahki
Rough-Face Girl's older sister

Pules
Rough-Face Girl's older sister

Rough-Face Girl
a strange-looking girl with a pure heart

SETTING

A large Indian village beside a lake

Storyteller: This is a tale from long ago. It tells of a strange-looking girl with a pure heart. She lived in a village beside a big lake.

Nootau: We are very lucky. A special being, called the Invisible One, lives at the edge of our village.

Invisible One: Only my sister, Nadie, can see me.

People of the village: No one else has ever seen the Invisible One.

Kanti: But I am sure he is handsome!

Kimi: He is also rich. And he has no wife, although he is looking for one!

Invisible One: My wife must be like me. She must always see and speak the truth.

Nootau: All the girls in our village want to be his wife. In order to do so, they must pass a test given by Nadie. Today, Kanti and Kimi are taking the test.

Nadie: Look over there. My brother is coming home from the hunt. Can you see him?

Kanti and **Kimi:** Yes!

Nadie: *(whispering)* Could these two be telling the truth? *(louder)* What is my brother's bow made of?

Kanti: Why, it is made of pure gold. And it shines like the sun!

Kimi: No, no! It is made of strong wood. That's what real bows are made of!

Nadie: *(whispering)* They are both wrong. They cannot see him. But I must be sure. *(louder)* Look again! What does my brother use to pull his sled?

Kanti: Why, a huge silver bear pulls his sled!

Kimi: How silly! He uses four dogs. Dogs pull sleds, not bears!

Nadie: No! No! You are both wrong. You have failed the test.

People: All the girls have failed!

Nootau: But my three girls have not taken the test yet. There is Tahki, my oldest. Then there is Pules, the middle child. We call the youngest one Rough-Face Girl.

Storyteller: You may wonder at her name. Nootau lost his wife long ago. Now his girls care for the home. In truth, only the youngest does any work.

Tahki: *(whispering)* It's true. We tell Rough-Face Girl that we have work to do by the lake.

Pules: Then we just sit and talk and laugh all day!

Tahki: Our trusting sister always does as she's told. Her main job is to sit by the fire and make sure it does not go out.

Pules: The sparks fly onto her face, arms, and hands. It's not our fault! We did not give her the scars!

Storyteller: From time to time, Nootau wonders if that is true . . .

Nootau: Why is my youngest the only one with scars?

Tahki: *(slyly)* She sits and dreams, Father. She does not see when the sparks fly. We are more careful and move out of the way.

Rough-Face Girl: *(softly)* That is true, Father. I do sometimes dream while I sit by the fire.

Storyteller: One day, Tahki and Pules came to their father.

Tahki: I want to take the test to wed the Invisible One. But I need a new beaded dress and new shoes. I must look my best for my new husband.

Pules: Me, too! My clothes must be as fine as Tahki's!

Nootau: I will give you what I can. But I must save something for Rough-Face Girl.

Pules: Oh, but her ugly scars make her shy. She won't want to go!

Tahki: She is a good worker. She'll be a fine wife for someone ... but not for the Invisible One.

Nootau: *(sighing)* Perhaps you are right.

Storyteller: And so it was. A few days later, Tahki and Pules sashayed through the village in their beautiful new clothes.

People: They are fine girls!

Nadie: *(whispering)* They may look fine on the outside, but on the inside they are cruel. I know their lying hearts. But I will take them to my brother. *(louder)* Can you see him?

Tahki and **Pules:** Of course!

Invisible One: They do not speak the truth. They do not see me. They do not hear me.

Nadie: *(whispering)* I must keep testing them, my brother. *(louder)* What is his bow made of?

Tahki: A strong piece of rawhide.

Pules: Um . . . yes . . . rawhide.

Nadie: And what does he use to pull his sled?

Tahki: *(whispering)* I think this is a trick question. *(louder)* Nothing! He pulls it himself, since he is so strong!

Pules: Oh, I don't think he could do that. Um . . . two deer? Four deer?

Nadie: Neither of you can see him! *Leave us!*

Storyteller: Finally, Rough-Face Girl found her courage. She went to her father.

Rough-Face Girl: Father, I would like to take the test. May I have a new dress?

Nootau: *(sighing)* I did not think you would want to go, my child. I have nothing to give you!

Rough-Face Girl: Do not feel bad. It is my fault. I should have told you before now. *(bravely)* No matter. I will find something!

Storyteller: So she made a strange dress from bark and leaves and bits of cloth. Then she hurried through the village.

People, Kanti, and **Kimi:** Ha! Ha! Such an odd girl!

Nadie: *(whispering)* This girl may look odd on the outside, but she is pure of heart. She may be the one. I will take her to my brother. *(louder)* You, the one called Rough-Face Girl. Can you see the Invisible One?

Rough-Face Girl: Why, yes! And what a regal figure he is!

Invisible One: *(whispering)* I think she sees me, sister!

Nadie: What is his bow made of?

Rough-Face Girl: Why, it is a rainbow!

Invisible One: She's right!

Nadie: What does he use to pull his sled?

Rough-Face Girl: He uses the stars that spill across the sky—the stars in the Milky Way!

Invisible One: Yes, yes, I do! She is the one, Nadie! Make her ready to be my wife.

Nadie: You have seen the truth and told the truth. You have passed the test! Come with me, dear girl. I will bathe you in my healing waters.

Storyteller: Nadie took the girl home. She washed away Rough-Face Girl's scars. She combed her hair and dressed her in luxurious clothes.

Nadie: You have always been lovely on the inside, dear girl. Now you are just as lovely on the outside. Come, my brother is waiting.

Invisible One: You can see and hear me, can't you?

Rough-Face Girl: *(softly)* Yes, I can.

Invisible One: From now on, I shall call you Nuttah. It means "my heart."

Storyteller: And so they were wed. All the people of the village were invited to the celebration.

People: They are a fine pair!

Nootau: My dearest daughter. I am so happy!

Tahki, Pules, Kanti, and **Kimi:** How did she know what to say?

Nadie: Silly girls. You still don't understand! You cannot lie to get your heart's desire. You must be true to yourself.

The End